Homecoming

K. RODRIGUEZ

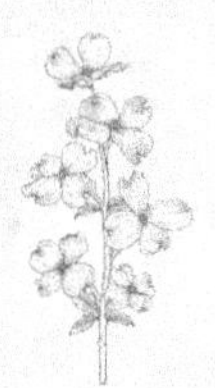

Homecoming

Returning to Haven, North Carolina, was supposed to be tempo-
rary—a quick stop to arrange care for my estranged father, who's
done little to deserve it. But instead of closure, I've reopened
wounds I thought years of therapy had healed…

It hasn't.

And then there's Julian. The boy I gave everything to in a single
week—the boy my father kicked me out over, twelve years ago.
He's still here, and the sparks between us are just as volatile.

I'd hoped to manage my past without getting burned, but Julian
remembers that night just as vividly as I do.

Learning to navigate the delicate balance of care and confrontation
with my dad is hard enough, but when the boy I left behind has
turned into the man I can't resist, every moment with him feels
like finding my way back home.

So, how do I leave when it's starting to feel like exactly where I
belong?

 Formatted with Vellum

Contents

One

"KAROLINA CASTILLO?"

"This is her," I reply quickly, eager to end the call. The professionalism in her tone does raise alarms in my head but not enough to tear me from my computer screen. I'm deep into writing my latest romance novel, racing against my publisher's revision deadline, and I've been in a rut all week—until inspiration struck an hour or so ago. Now, I can't tear my fingers away from the keys to focus on this unexpected call that I most definitely did not mean to answer.

"This is Eve Thompson, a nurse here at Haven Medical Center. I'm calling regarding your father, Sergio Castillo?"

My fingers freeze, and my breath hitches in my throat. The letters on my screen jumble together as I'm yanked from the vibrant world I'd just created and thrust back into the harsh reality of life.

. . .

"Yes," is all I can manage. A knot twists in my stomach, squeezing tight. I brace myself for whatever news is coming, trying to remind myself that it is what it is. The state of our relationship was his undoing, not mine and I've made peace with that.

That's not what your therapist says.

"Your father's been in an accident. He's stable, but his injuries are significant. The doctors have him in a medically induced coma for the moment, to help him heal and evaluate the extent of his injuries. I understand you live out of state. You might wanna make arrangements to get here as soon as you can so the doctors can discuss everything with you further."

"Okay," I reply, my mind struggling to grasp the weight of the situation.

"Do you need our address?"

I shake my head, realizing too late that she can't see me. "No, I know my way home. Thank you," I add before disconnecting the call.

Home?

. . .

Haven, North Carolina hasn't been my home since I was nine. The name feels foreign, and I can't even recall the last time I thought about it or my dad—except for the occasional therapy session where both have been the root of many discussions.

I shut my laptop and head out of my home office to my bedroom, grabbing my suitcase from the linen closet. I pack quickly, tossing shorts and leggings into my bag when I remember where the hell I'm going and how unprepared I am for the drastic weather change.

Glancing out the window at the warm Tampa sunshine filtering in, you would realize we were deep into fall here if it weren't for pumpkin spice being in season. The vibrant colors of autumn are lost here, replaced by palm trees, humidity, and endless blue skies.

So how do I pack for a place that feels like a distant memory?

I rummage through my closet for sweaters I reserve mostly for the brutal air of indoor A/C and layerable items. I toss my toiletries in and zip up my suitcase, noticing the tremble in my fingers. My heart pounding as anxiety coils around my thoughts like a vine.

I take a deep breath, forcing the tightness in my chest to ease. My mind racing with a thousand "what ifs," but I push them aside. No time for tears or regret right now. I shake my head and focus. I pull out my phone and search for Haven Medical Center and enter it into my navigation app.

. . .

Nine hours and twenty-two minutes—that's six hundred and thirty-six miles until I reach my destination. If I leave now, I'll get there by ten tonight. I grab the sports jacket I left on my bed when Zorro, my black cat, jumps up onto my bed. He meows at me, as if asking 'And where do you think you're going, young lady?' Of course, I imagine him saying this with an accent as thick as Antonio Banderas.

I rub his chin, smiling as he arches into my touch and begins to purr.

"I know you don't like it when I leave, but I'll be back as soon as I can. I just need to make sure he's okay until he wakes up, and then I'm hauling ass back here. Promise." He jumps down and I follow him out as he walks into the kitchen. "Let's make sure you have plenty of food and water while I'm gone, but you know Mami will be here checking in on you." I fill his automatic food dispenser and two-liter stainless steel water fountain. He rubs against my leg before darting over to his lavish floor-to-ceiling cat penthouse, complete with multiple levels, plush bedding, and even a built-in scratching post.

Zorro may be a rescue, but my baby is bougie.

I continue talking to him because honestly, I have yet to meet a man who listens like he does. "I'll wait until I'm on the road to call Mom or you know she'll try to convince me to fly there—or worse, try to come with me." He meows back as if to say, "Girl, I don't blame you," while rolling onto his side.

. . .

I pack a canvas bag with snacks for the drive and a couple of energy drinks before shouting, "Love you, bye!" to Zorro and heading out.

As I lock the door, memories of the last time I made this drive flood my mind. I had come down on a whim during summer break before starting college after my dad surprised me by flying down for my high school graduation. It was a rare visit since all we had shared since the divorce were Sunday morning phone calls. The naive teenage girl with clear-cut daddy issues yearned for more from him.

But instead of the bonding experience I had hoped for, it spiraled into the biggest mistake of my life—one that ended with my father kicking me out of his house and me giving my virginity to the boy next door.

God, I was such a mess.

Two

"IN FIVE HUNDRED FEET, TURN RIGHT."

The loud voice of the GPS cuts through the music that, along with the cans of energy drinks in my passenger seat, has been keeping me awake for the last hour. I'm in the home stretch—literally just half a mile to go—but it feels like the longest part of the drive. What was supposed to be a nine-hour trip has stretched into over thirteen after hitting rush hour traffic in Atlanta and wasting an additional thirty minutes stopping for gas.

As I focus on the pitch-black surroundings, I reach for the energy drink in my cupholder and tilt my head back, hoping for at least a drop to keep me awake for the rest of this drive without crashing into a tree. Just as I turn right, down the street from my dad's, I catch a glimpse of movement out of the corner of my eye and slam on my brakes as a jogger emerges from the shadows, dressed in dark clothing with thick headphones covering his ears.

. . .

My tires skid slightly as I come to an abrupt stop, my heart racing. The guy stumbles to the side, and I can barely make out his silhouette before rolling down my window and apologizing profusely.

"I'm so sorry! I didn't see you at all. Are you okay?"

I can feel his stare but can't make out his face; he doesn't respond. I hit the lock button and hover my finger over the window button.

"Okay, you be safe, and I'm really sorry again."

I drive off slowly, keeping the stranger in my rearview mirror.

"Your destination will be to your left."

A sigh of relief escapes me as the driveway comes into view, and I slide into one of the two parking spots beside my dad's house. I put the car in park and relax into my seat, grateful to finally be off the road. But when I glance back into my rearview mirror, I see the stranger I nearly hit just moments ago now running up my dad's driveway.

Panic courses through me, jolting me into action. Without thinking twice, I open the glove compartment and grab the pepper spray I've never had to use but always feel better having within reach. My heart pounds as I take the safety off, the need to protect myself overtaking my thoughts. My dad isn't home to help, and at nearly two in the morning, the chances of any Good Samaritan being around are slim.

I fling open my driver's door, stepping out into the cold November air. I shiver in my thin jacket as the jogger approaches.

"Stay back!" I shout, my voice trembling as I press my thumb down on the trigger, sending a stream of spray in his direction.

"What the fuck, Lina? Is that mace?" He stumbles back, his hands instinctively reaching up to shield his face.

I stand frozen in place. "How do you know my name?" I shout. He ignores me, gasping as he trips over the lawn, making a beeline for the hose coiled against the side of the house. A floodlight by the back door flickers on, illuminating him as rushing water fills the air and he frantically splashes it onto his face.

He lifts the hose over his head, letting the water run down.

Realization suddenly hits me at who I just pepper-sprayed.

The new neighbor I had met all those years ago—and the one night we spent together—fills my mind. "Julian?" I ask in disbelief.

As I tuck the mace into my pocket, I take a step forward suddenly needing a better look at him.

He's bigger than I remember, with broad shoulders that fill out his sweater, hinting at the toned arms beneath that I don't recall him having before.

It's been ten years, Lina. Of course, he's taken better care of himself than the nineteen-year-old he once was.

And I just maced him.

I cringe at the thought, wrapping my arms around myself as I take a few hesitant steps closer.

"I had no idea it was you. I am so sorry."

He shifts slightly, turning off the hose, and stares at me with an intensity that sends a chill down my spine, the glimmer of red in his eyes cutting through the dim light.

"You said that before when you nearly ran me over," he replies, clearly irritated.

"And I apologize again. It's been a really long day, and that drive was so much harder than I remember." I pause, frustration suddenly bubbling inside of me. "What were you even doing out at this time? You need, like, reflective gear or something—and maybe a sign that says you come in peace!"

"Noted," he replies, a hint of sarcasm in his voice. "I wish I could say it's good to see you, Lina, but so far, it's almost killed me." He walks past me toward his house next door.

"I said I was sorry!" I call out again, my voice trailing off.

With a heavy sigh, I grab my bags from my car, shuffling through my key ring for the copy he gave me all those years ago, back when we hoped to make my visits more frequent.

Once inside, I'm shocked at how time seems to have stood still in the cramped living room that suddenly feels smaller than ever. The overwhelming scent of his cologne clings to the air, wrapping around me and holding me in a chokehold as unbidden tears fill my eyes.

Nope. I cannot sleep here.

I leave my suitcase in the corner of the living room and head back toward my car, opting for the front seat instead. Once I'm settled in, I gaze out the darkened window, staring up at the house next door. My mind drifts back to that night so long ago and the boy I spent it with, wondering what would have happened if things had turned out differently.

Three

SLEEPING in my car was a terrible idea. I was freezing cold and my mind would not turn off. By the time sleep finally found me, the morning light was streaming in through all of the windows, leaving me no other choice but to start my day.

From the words of a very wise woman; "Primero cafecito" but first, coffee.

I do a quick Google search and find the nearest drive-thru coffee shop. It's not as close as I'd like, but it's a far better start to the day than this.

Once I'm caffeinated and back at my dad's I shower and get ready for the day, feeling more human and less grumpy cat. I settle onto the couch for a minute when I realize my phone has no service which is no surprise out here in the boonies. I start hunting for the internet router, hoping the wifi password is written somewhere nearby. To my surprise it's taped right on top: MrPlatano-Power809.

. . .

A smile instantly spreads across my face as I type it into my phone to connect when my phone buzzes with a slew of missed calls and texts from my mom. Suddenly it rings in my hand with an incoming call from her. I didn't call her last night or this morning, so I can already imagine the tongue-lashing she has in store for me.

"Hi, Mom."

"Don't you 'hi, Mom' me. What time did you get in?"

"Almost two, and I went right to bed."

"I figured. Have you seen your dad yet?"

"No. I checked the visiting hours yesterday, and they don't start until nine, so I have some time."

"Are you sure you don't want me to fly up there?"

"No, Mom. You two were awkward enough the last time you had to share the same space. It's fine. I'll see him today, get him set up with an aide or something to help him, and then I'll be on my way."

. . .

"Lina," she says, her tone softening.

"Ma, I have some work to get to before I head over to the hospital, okay? I'll call you later."

"Okay, mi hija."

"Don't forget about Zorro, please."

"I could never. He's as close to a grandson as I'm going to get. Te quiero, chao."

"Love you."

We hang up, and open my laptop, ditching writing for a social media hunt of a certain brewdy neighbor.

Two hours later, I'm sitting in my car, parked in front of Haven Medical Center, where I've been for the last thirty minutes. I can't seem to make myself walk in. I've watched countless people come and go, but the longer I sit here, the harder it gets to open this door and take that first step.

A tap at my window pulls me from my staring match with the entrance. I turn to see Julian standing there, hands tucked into the front pockets of his sweatshirt, brows furrowed as he studies me.

In the full light of day, I can't help but notice how much he's changed. The easygoing boy I once knew has been replaced by this broody version. The seriousness in his glare makes me swallow the lump lodged in my throat.

I press the button to lower the window a crack.

"You okay?" he asks, his deep voice a smooth rasp compared to the edge of tension it held last night.

I nod, afraid my mouth will betray the jumble of thoughts swirling in my mind. Anxiety knots in my stomach as my grip tightens on the steering wheel at the thought of seeing my dad again after so long. Twelve years of silence have passed since the venom we both hurled at each other that night. The unresolved pain I thought I had moved past hangs heavy in my heart.

"Do you want to walk in together? I can take you straight to his room so you don't have to go looking for it."

"I would appreciate that, yes." I nod again but make no move to get out of the car.

Julian opens the car door and kneels down beside me, his scent—a mix of cedar and something warm—fills the small space between us. I turn to face him, and his eyes search mine, making my heart race. All can do is breathe him in as he reaches over, prying my fingers from the steering wheel and holding them in his hands.

. . .

"It's not as bad as you're thinking right now," he says softly. "He's a fighter; he always has been. He'll make it through this, okay? And he'll be happy to see you. Trust me."

His words wrap around me, easing some of the tension inside as I cling to the hope that maybe, even after everything,it could be true.

Taking a deep breath, I respond, "Okay, okay." and wipe the tears from the corners of my eyes, feeling embarrassment flood over me for crying in front of him. "Sorry about all of this."

"You keep apologizing," he replies gently, a hint of a smile playing on his lips.

"Sor—" I clamp my mouth shut as he narrows his eyes at me.

"Are you ready?" he asks, standing and reaching his hand out for me to take.

"As ready as I'll ever be," I respond, taking his hand.

He doesn't move back as I exit the car and stand in front of him. Our chests brush, and his lips are close enough that I can smell the mint on his breath.

. . .

"It is really good to see you, Lina. Even if you'll be the death of me."

"Ditto,"

"Come on," he mutters, shutting my car door behind me and releasing my hand. The sudden loss of his warm touch washes over me as a cold gust rushes by, making me shiver. I reach into the warmth of my jacket pocket and press the lock button on the key fob, the sound of my car locking echoing behind us as we cross the parking lot.

Julian easily guides us through the hospital, nodding to staff who wave at him as we make our way to the elevator. When we reach the hallway toward my dad's room, the sound of his laughter wafts out, causing me to stall in my tracks.

He's awake.

Four

"HEY, old man. Look what I found in the parking lot," Julian says, pulling me behind him.

The nurse at my father's bedside moves over, and for the first time in twelve years, I meet my father's eyes. Tears instantly fill my eyes as I take in his bruised and battered face. His leg is propped up and bandaged, while his arm is in a sling over his chest.

"Karolina?" he sucks in a breath.

"Dad," I whisper, holding back a sob. I thought I wouldn't care. I thought I'd be numb. But I'm just so grateful to see him in one piece.

In the next second, I'm by his side, careful not to disturb the IVs in his free hand. I gently intertwine our fingers and give a soft squeeze as his eyes lock onto mine, wide with disbelief.

"Am I still sleeping?" he asks.

I shake my head, tears falling down my face. "No, it's me, Dad. I'm sorry. I'm so sorry it took me so long to come back. That it took this–"

"No, no, no, mi corazón. Perdóname." No, no, no, my heart. Forgive me. I've regretted that night every day since," he says, his voice shaking.

"I was so stupid, Dad," I reply, choking on my words. The weight of that argument, heavy and suffocating, crashes over me as the floodgates I've forced closed finally open.

"Ya, ya, mi corazón," he says, wiping my tears with the pad of his thumb. "We both made mistakes. It's in the past. Now," he pauses, lifting my hand and smiling with pride, "let me look at my daughter, New York Times bestselling author Karolina Castillo." He says my name like an announcer, and I can't help but laugh through my tears.

Julian and the nurse break into applause, their smiles brightening the sterile room. My eyes, however, can't help but bounce back to Julian. His smile catches me off guard, sending a jolt through me.

. . .

I force my gaze back to my dad, the reason I'm here in the first place.

"Lina, I've heard so much about you," the nurse beside Julian says, offering a gentle smile as she walks up to me and places a hand on my shoulder. "I'm so glad you were able to make it so soon." She gives my shoulder a gentle squeeze before continuing. Her warm, rich voice has a soothing Southern drawl that instantly puts me at ease. I realize she must be the nurse I spoke with the day before. "Julian mentioned your fear of flying, and I wasn't sure how long the drive from Florida would take you. I'm Eve; we spoke on the phone." She extends her hand to shake.

"Yes," I say, shaking her hand. "Thank you so much for calling me."

"Of course, sweetheart. I've known Sergio for a while, and I knew how much having you here would mean to him when he woke up, no matter what Julian here said." She purses her lips and lowers her thick red frames to the tip of her nose while giving Julian a knowing look.

"And what did he say?" I ask, turning my attention back to Julian, who is now scratching the back of his head and avoiding my gaze as he takes a seat at the end of my father's bed. His expression unreadable.

Eve chuckles softly, sensing the tension. "Oh, just that you might be a little hesitant about making the trip. But I knew you'd come through for your dad. That's what family does, no matter the strife in between."

"You being here means everything to me, Lina. Gracias," Dad says.

"I'll leave you two to catch up. I'm glad to see you in one piece, Viejo," Julian says..

"Viejo, my ass, punk," Dad replies, throwing a playful punch in the air toward Julian, who dramatically pretends to dodge it.

"Okay, boys. Let's not start a brawl in here," Eve laughs, shaking her head. "Let's not add to your already extensive list of injuries, Serg. The doctor should be in soon to see you. "

"Yes, ma'am," they say in unison, and I can't help but smile at their playful banter. Twelve years ago, my dad wanted to kill Julian, and now it seems like they're best friends.

Eve says goodbye, and Julian follows her out. The sheepish glance he gives me before turning down the hallway makes my stomach flutter.

Damn it.

. . .

Dad and I try to catch up on as much as we can before the doctor comes in. He fills me in on the accident and how lucky my dad was to just have a couple of broken bones. He details the recovery plan, which will entail close monitoring of the concussion he suffered and physical therapy for at least three to six months. He'll need to stay in the hospital for a few more days, which gives me plenty of time to get the house ready for him.

Five

AS I STEP out of the hospital, I take a deep breath, mentally checking off the list of things my dad will need once he's home when a cool breeze hits me, sending a familiar shiver through my body. I glance around the parking lot, feeling as though I'm being watched, and then spot Julian leaning against the hood of his car parked beside mine.

"Looking for more ways to die?" Instantly cringing at how dumb that sounded. God, why am I like this?

"What?" he asks, his eyebrows knitting together in confusion.

"It sounded better in my head," I admit, wincing.

Julian chuckles, the sound easily bringing a smile to my lips as I stare up at him.

. . .

"You hungry?" A playful smirk tugs at the corner of his lips.

I nod.

"Come on." He pushes himself off the hood and opens the passenger side of his car. I swallow the lump in my throat before stepping onto the running board, his hands finding my hips to help me up.

"Sweet Haven, okay? Or are you in the mood for something else?" he asks as soon as he jumps in.

Definitely in the mood for you.

"Sweet Haven is good," I reply, my voice coming out a little higher than intended. I give him a tight smile that betrays the thoughts racing through my mind with him so close, the cab of the truck smelling so much like him.

He narrows his eyes, as if sensing my internal battle. "Are you sure? A lot has changed since you were last here. We've got an Outback now."

"Wow. Little old Haven is coming up, huh?"

. . .

"She sure is," he says.

"But there's only one Sweet Haven Diner."

"Damn right," he replies, turning the key and bringing his truck to life.

The sound of the engine fills the silence that suddenly falls between us lingering until I can't take another second of it.

"So, you really thought I'd just ignore my dad after his accident?"

"Just getting right to it?" He asks, staring ahead. .

"I mean, it was hard not to notice the death glare Eve was giving you. Must have been some argument you had to convince her I wouldn't come."

"It's been twelve years, Lina."

"And? He's my dad, Julian. What kind of monster do you think I am to ignore the call about his accident? Did you expect me to just send flowers to his bedside?"

"No, that's not—" He sighs. "I know how complicated things are between you two. I didn't want you to feel obligated to come up here. Besides, he's had my back more times than I can count. I owe him."

"Since when have you two been close, anyway? Last time I saw him, he wanted to drag you through Main Street."

"People change, Lina. Time will do that, you know?"

I turn my head and look out the window, starting to regret getting into his car as Haven passes by.

We pull into the diner's parking lot, the neon red sign flickering in the early evening light, flooding me with nostalgia.

Julian parks the truck and turns to me.

"I'm sorry. I should have known better than to doubt you'd be here for your dad. You always had a way of proving me wrong. Guess I just forgot."

"I guess I'll just have to remind you."

"I guess so." He gazes at my lips.

. . .

Electricity courses under my skin stirring wisps of a memory that feels more like a dream. But the sound of a car door slamming shut snaps us back to reality. Julian blinks a few times, shaking his head as if the spell has been lifted. He climbs out leaving me breathless and confused but just his proximity.

I know without a doubt I am in trouble.

Inside the diner, it's like walking straight into the 1950s, with its bright red vinyl booths and checkered floor. Aside from a few new faces, even the staff looks familiar, though older.

I follow Julian to a booth in the back and sit across from him, my eyes darting around the room to avoid his gaze as we wait for the waitress.

"So, what have you been up to besides starting a bromance with my father?" I tease.

"Oh, you know, same old same old."

"Which is?"

He shrugs as if not knowing where to start, "I enlisted in the army not long after you left. One tour in Afghanistan was enough for me, and I came back here. Laid low for a while, kept myself busy, started buying and flipping houses, and realized I really like working with my hands."

I can't help but look down at those hands, remembering how well they worked me.

"Hey, Julian!" the waitress calls from behind me as she walks up to our booth. "I'm so happy to catch you here today. Any news on Sergio?" she asks, stopping beside me. I realize it's Judy, the same waitress who worked here since I was a kid.

"He's awake and doing well. The doc said it would be, what, another week before he comes home?" He pauses, looking at me.

"Just a few more days, actually," I finish. Judy finally notices me, her eyes widening with realization.

"Goodness gracious, Lina! Oh, look at you!" She suddenly turns her head, shouting into the direction of the kitchen. "Henry! Henry! Come out here! You won't believe who's here!"

I smile, embarrassed, as everyone in the diner notices us, and I can't avoid the hushed whispers in our direction.

There's a commotion from the back of the kitchen as an older man comes out, looking annoyed at being called out. He stops in his tracks when he sees me. I give him a small wave, and he smiles wide, his thick black mustache covering his front teeth.

"Well, I'll be damned. If it isn't Little Lina! I used to make you special banana pudding milkshakes. Do you still like those? I can whip one up for you right now."

I chuckle happily at his sweet offer and take him up on it, watching him rush back to make it. The rest of our time turns into a reunion of sorts, with neighbors of my dad's—people who watched me grow up before I left with my mom—stopping by our table to say hello. After Julian and I place our order, Judy shows me the framed pictures on the wall: a printout of my New York Times bestseller, a photo of me sitting on a stool at Sweet Haven as a child, and another framed picture of my headshot, which I offer to sign.

I feel so honored by this little corner of Sweet Haven's wall. It takes me back to how excited I used to get when my mom hung my art projects on the fridge. It hits me all of a sudden that I've always had a place here. With or without this wall, this is home.

Six

DINNER TAKES FOREVER to get through, but I don't mind—especially when Judy offers to put together a little welcome-home dinner for Dad at the diner when he gets back. Feeling beyond grateful for this tight-knit community, it's like I'm seeing them all for the first time. I can understand why Dad has stayed in Haven; this isn't something you can find anymore.

Julian and I don't get to talk much, which may be for the best considering where my thoughts are going. He drives me back to the hospital to pick up my car, and he's quiet during most of the drive, feeling more like the stranger I maced the other night. When he pulls into the spot beside my car, I've got my seatbelt off and my hand on the door handle before he stops me.

"I hate to admit how much I've thought about you since—" His eyes skim down my face and land on my mouth. The soft shadows cast by the parking lot light illuminate his brown eyes, making them look like embers in the dark. We both know exactly what he means by "since."

"Then don't admit it."

"Why not?"

"Because it's a bad idea, Julian. Thanks for dinner." I climb out of his truck, slamming the door harder than intended before jumping into mine. I start the engine and breathe a sigh of relief as Julian pulls out of his spot, then cover my face with my hands. I cannot be doing this with him. It's a bad idea. At least when we gave in to our attraction before, we could blame it on being young and dumb —but we know better now. I'm here for Dad and then going back home to Florida.

I take my time driving to my dad's, hoping to avoid arriving at the same time as Julian. Of course, just as I park the car, his truck pulls up the driveway, reversing right into the spot beside me. Not in the mood for a confrontation, I rush out of my car before he turns off the engine, but by the time I reach the door, I can hear the crunch of gravel beneath his shoes as he follows me.

"Lina," he calls out. I tell myself not to do it, but I stop anyway, my heart begging me to turn around.

"Julian, please."

. . .

"Why'd you leave?"

I freeze. "What?"

"Why did you leave before?"

"I don't know what you're talking about. Just go home and forget this."

"You're really going to act like that night meant nothing to you? You didn't even tell me I was your first, and by the time I realized, you were gone."

"We're not doing this."

"That's right. Go ahead and run, Lina. That's what you're so good at. I shouldn't expect anything less than the back of your head."

"I don't need this, Julian. This isn't what I drove all this way for."

"Tell me that night meant nothing to you, and I'll turn around right now. I won't bring it up again."

I force a laugh, hoping it sounds more convincing than it feels. "It was one night twelve years ago."

. . .

"It's not about that night but the girl I spent it with."

"That girl isn't here anymore," I whisper.

"Bullshit." Before I can react, his lips are on mine, his hands slipping past my curls and behind my neck, lifting my head to meet his mouth. His kiss is desperate, as if he's been starved for years. I thread my fingers into the top of his curls, pulling him closer. The rest of the world disappears—the anger, the pain, the cold night—replaced by the undeniable heat that's always been between us.

""Tell me it meant nothing to you. That you haven't thought about me once." He swallows hard, using all his strength to keep from kissing me again, but the need is overwhelming, and I'm trembling.

I glide my hand over his heart, gripping the collar of his jacket. I open my mouth, but the lie thick on my tongue gets caught in my throat. The intensity in his eyes takes my breath away. I shake my head and whisper, "I can't."

In the next moment, his mouth is crashing into mine, igniting a fire that makes me forget all about the cold air around us. His arms pull me into him, effortlessly lifting me off my feet as his tongue plunges into my mouth, slowly colliding with mine. He walks us backward until my back presses against the wall of my dad's house, and I quickly dive into my pockets for the key.

．　．　．

Once inside, Julian easily guides us through the house while we make quick work of peeling off our clothes, dropping them on the floor on our way to my bedroom, our kiss growing more desperate with each layer we remove. I thread my fingers into the top of his curls as he lowers me onto the bed, not wanting to break this kiss for anything.

Everything around us fades away—the anger, the pain, and the years between us—replaced by the undeniable heat that's always been there as we explore each other's bodies, etching every inch into memory.

SOFT MORNING LIGHT filters through my childhood curtains, the pink butterflies and sun casting the room in a warm glow. For a moment, I forget where I am and when, until I take a deep breath, filling my senses with Julian's warm cedar scent mixed with traces of me. His arm drapes over me, radiating heat, while his warm breath against my neck sends a chill down my spine. Living in Florida for so long, you'd think I'd be used to the heat, but this is different—he's different—consuming me and igniting me from the inside out.

Memories of the night before rush in, a smile lifting the corners of my lips as my body comes alive, recalling the fire in our touch, as if we were both trying to etch another memory into our hearts. But suddenly, a wave of anxiety crashes over me, and as my mind tries to bring me back to my senses. I try to pry myself free, but the reality of our situation settles in—regret and desire battling it out in my heart, while the fear of the past repeating itself wins. Here I am in Haven for my dad, just like before, and Julian should be nothing more than a footnote from my past. We were a blip in each other's lives for barely five seconds, yet here he is, trying to hijack the whole story.

I have responsibilities and a timeline here. I'm getting Dad set up with a home nurse, and then I'm back on the road before the end of the month. Dad and I can pick up on our Sunday phone calls and maybe even more. If I can convince him to come to Florida, that would be even better, but I can't promise more than that. I have a whole life to get back to—deadlines, signings, and book deals. I can't do that from here with Mom.

Julian and I— we can't—this can't be anything more than this.

Gently, I shift away from him, careful not to wake him, and roll onto my knees. My heart races as I crawl, bare-assed naked, toward the door.

"What are you doing?"

I freeze at the sound of his voice, rough with sleep.

As if sensing my inner turmoil, Julian sits up, the sheets pooling in front of him. His bare chest and the tattoos I couldn't see in the dark, now illuminated by the morning light. It's a beautiful work of art I can't look away from, no matter how foolish I feel right now.

. . .

He narrows his eyes, the anger in them holding me hostage as I rack my brain for words.

He climbs out of bed, and I'm grateful he has his boxers on—because I can see this playing out in so many different ways, each one ending with me on all fours, forgetting all about my escape.

He walks slowly toward me, kneeling down in front of me, his finger tipping my chin up so I can't look away. "I'm only going to ask you once more, Lina. What are you doing?"

His words vibrate through me. I swallow hard, searching for the courage to say what needs to be said.

"You were leaving," he says, exhaling slowly.

The sound of my phone ringing in the other room jolts me into action. I grab a crumpled t-shirt closest to me and tug it on, noticing too late that it's definitely Julian's before rushing out to grab my phone, still in my jacket pocket.

"Haven Medical Center" flashes on the screen.

"Hello," I answer, though my ears are more focused on Julian moving around in my bedroom. He emerges from the room, half-dressed in his jeans and sneakers, probably searching for the t-shirt I'm currently wrapped in.

. . .

"Lina, it's Eve. I know it's early, but I just clocked in for my shift and—" She pauses. "He had a stroke last night."

"What?" Dread pools in my stomach as I fall onto the couch. Julian is instantly by my side, watching me. "Is he okay?"

"He's stable, but after a scan, the doctor found some concerning signs. He wants to talk to you in person if you can head down."

"I'll be right there."

I hang up and scramble around the room, searching for my sneakers.

"Lina?" Julian asks, concern lacing his voice. "What happened?"

"He had a stroke, and the scan—" Tears fill my eyes as the rest of the words get stuck in my throat. Julian pulls me into his arms, and I shake my head, pushing against him. "I have to go."

"Just take a minute, okay?" He slips a hand behind my neck, urging me to stay put.

"I can't do this with you."

. . .

"We're not doing anything. Just take a minute, stay with me. That's it."

I breathe in and out, letting my head fall against his chest as I wrap my arms around him. His fingers trace a path up and down my neck until my shallow breaths even out.

"You don't have to go through this alone. I'm here. I've been here, and your dad means more to me than anyone else." His words make my heart ache.

"I'm scared," I admit. "What if I let all these wasted years go by, and yesterday is all we have left?"

"Don't do that. Don't let your mind go there."

"You're right, sor—" He pins me with a glare. "Look, I came back to support my dad, and I can't let anything get in the way of that. Not even you." Tears prick at my eyes as I bite my tongue to keep myself from saying anything else.

Like, I want you. I need you. I've only ever come to life when I'm in your arms, and I don't want to take just another memory of us back home.

. . .

His jaw clenches, and I can see understanding flicker in his eyes. He nods and untangles himself from me, my skin instantly missing his warmth.

"You need pants," he says, looking down at my bare legs. "Get dressed, and I'll drive you."

"You don't have to. I can—"

He cuts me off. "We can support each other right now. You don't have to choose."

But the truth is I've chosen once before. I chose Haven, I chose Julian, and I chose moving back in with my dad to start fresh. At the time, it felt like a win-win, but that quickly turned sideways when my dad caught me sneaking into the house after my night with Julian and then smashed those dreams to pieces.

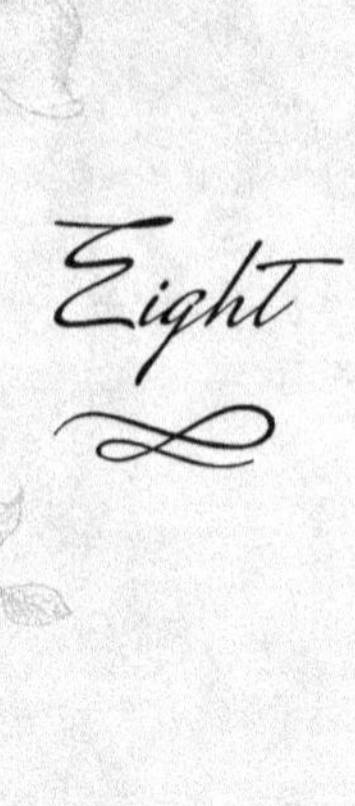

Eight

THE DRIVE to the hospital blurs into a haze as Julian navigates the roads as quickly as he can. The silence between us hangs heavy in the air. My leg bounces nervously as I pick at the skin on the corner of my nail until Julian's hand covers mine, instantly calming my frayed nerves. I glance up, studying him as he keeps his gaze fixed on the road ahead, his jaw clenched and brows furrowed while gripping the steering wheel tightly with his other hand.

I follow his gaze out the windshield toward a still-sleeping Haven, oblivious to the storm raging inside me. Hot tears burn my vision as I regret not coming back sooner—before the accident, when we still had time.

"Lina," Julian's voice is steady but low, breaking through my thoughts as we come to a stop at a red light. I turn my head, surprised to find him staring back at me, his eyes warm and full of concern. "You still have time." He squeezes my hand as the light turns green.

. . .

I nod and squeeze back, grateful for his presence right now, wanting to reassure him as well. He's the one who's been here after all, spending time I should have been with my dad.

"You never told me how you and my dad got close?"

He chuckles softly. "It was after my deployment, after my grandma passed and left me the house. I was a mess, trying to figure out what to do next while my head still felt buried in the sand. I was broken, lost, and alone. A lot of people I considered family turned away from me, and then your dad showed up with his toolbox and a can of paint, talking about the condition of my grandmother's home. Next thing I knew, we were redoing the siding and painting the walls. When it was all done, he was still there, checking up on me. He'd talk about you, your books, and the pieces of you buried in different characters.."

"He's read my books?" I ask, surprise flooding my voice.

"Read them? He learned how to annotate them after he came across one of your reader groups talking about it."

I can't help smiling through my tears at the thought of him now.

"Your dad and your books reminded me that as long as I found something or someone to hold on to, I could always find my way back."

"I'm glad he had you," I say softly, squeezing his hand.

"Me too."

As Julian pulls into the hospital parking lot, I tighten my grip on his hand, like he's my lifeline—the only thing keeping me from falling apart.

***

The doctor's words still echo in my head—"critical" and "surgery" —stuck on a loop as the sounds of the monitors and machines fade into the distance. Time feels like it's been at a standstill since this morning, and the surgery Dad needed dragged well into the afternoon. Now, all we can do is wait. That's what the doctor said, at least, but I don't think I can sit here staring at this pale, fragile version of my dad for another second.

My heart pounds harder in my chest with every second that passes, each one feeling like an hour, trapping me in this room. A tight knot forms in my stomach, twisting with each thought racing through my mind. What if he doesn't wake up? What if yesterday was all we had? What if—

. . .

"You need to eat," Julian says, walking into the room holding a takeout bag. The sweet smell of BBQ incites a vicious growl from my stomach, one I don't even recognize. But the idea of eating feels impossible with these nerves making me feel sick.

"Don't make that face," Julian says. "I could hear your stomach down the hall." He pops the lid open on one of the containers and forks out some pulled pork, leaning closer to hold it just in front of my lips.

"Open," he says, his voice almost a whisper as his gaze drops to my mouth.

I lean in just enough to take a bite, savoring the smoky flavor before pulling back. But I can't help glancing back at my dad's still-sleeping figure, guilt gnawing at me as I shake my head.

"No more." I say, pulling away as I chew the bit I have in my mouth. I lean back in the chair and wrap my arms around my knees, tucking them to my chest.

Julian sighs, setting the container aside. He rummages through the takeout bag, and I suddenly feel the urge to send him away.

"Fries?"

I shake my head.

. . .

"Your dad will kill me if he finds out I let you starve yourself for his sake."

"Damn right I will," my dad's voice, hoarse and gravelly, cuts through the air, shocking both Julian and me.

"Dad," I jump up, my heart racing as relief washes over me. I lean over him, wrapping my arms around him as best as I can, careful of all the wires attached to him. Julian steps closer, rubbing the tears from his own eyes before placing a hand on my dad's shoulder.

"You scared us there, old man."

"Punk," Dad replies, but the effort shows on his face, his words coming out slowly like a puff of air.

The hairs on the back of my neck raise as I notice him struggling to move his arms, his fingers twitching slightly.

"Do you feel okay?"

He looks at me, concern and fear filling his eyes as he tries to answer. "I... I'm..."

. . .

"I'll go grab the doctor," Julian whispers, rushing out of the room.

"Li-li-li—"

"It's okay." I try to reassure him, wrapping my hand over his and squeezing tight. His fingers twitch beneath mine. "I'm here. I'm not going anywhere, Dad."

Nine

BETWEEN TESTS, physical therapy, and rearranging the house for Dad's discharge, the weeks drag on, blending into one another with no end in sight. I've made myself at home in Dad's hospital room, and to my surprise—and my agent's delight—I've even managed to get some writing done.

The story I've been working on has taken an unexpected turn, and the male main character has surprisingly morphed into a certain stubborn, frustratingly sexy neighbor turned one—no, two— night stand. A man I've been trying to avoid, and luckily, he's been doing one hell of a job giving me space.

I shake my head, trying to focus on the road instead of on Julian. It's bad enough that he's hijacked my writing; I don't need to be obsessing over him in real life too.

My gaze drifts toward Dad, sitting quietly beside me in the passenger seat, staring out the window. The view of the mountains framing the horizon catches my eye for a moment, and I can't help but smile at the sight before turning back to the road.

"You okay, Dad?" I ask, glancing over.

He turns to me, smiling. "I love... these mountains." He says, his voice is strained, but it's so much better than it was a few weeks ago.

I smile back at him, my heart lifting to see him out of that hospital room.

"Me too. I haven't had a chance to cook or go grocery shopping yet. How about we stop for some dinner before heading home?" I ask, trying my best to sound as casual as possible while containing my excitement over the surprise party waiting for him at the diner.

"Sweet Haven?" he suggests, his eyes lighting up at the thought of his favorite little diner.

"Only if you promise to eat a salad on the side." I can't help teasing him.

He scrunches his nose in mock disgust. "Salad?"

. . .

"Yes, salad. Your tests showed high cholesterol, remember?"

He lets out a dramatic groan as I pull into the parking lot.

Sweet Haven is packed with cars, and I can't believe all these people are here for my dad. Once I help him out of the car, I shoot a quick text to Eve, letting her know we're walking in.

"Looks like the whole town is here tonight," I say, unable to hide my grin.

"It sure does, doesn't it?"

As soon as we swing the diner door open, a loud "Surprise!" fills the air, echoing off the walls and spilling out into the street behind us.

Dad instantly pulls me close, his grip strong despite the weeks of recovery. "What is this?" he murmurs, a touch of emotion breaking through his usual steady voice.

Before I can reply, he's swept up by a swarm of townspeople— some I recognize, most I don't. A hand lands gently on my shoulder, and I turn to find my mom standing beside me.

"Mom!" I cry out jumping into her arms.

. . .

"Mi amor," she says, squeezing me tight. "I've missed you so much! It's so weird being back here. And you have a whole wall!"

"I know," I laugh, embarrassed.

We quickly catch up on her flight in this morning and things back home when she remembers Zorro in his cat carrier. She runs off to grab him from the front counter, where she left him waiting, when suddenly the air shifts around me, and I know without a doubt why. My heart pounds a little harder in my chest as I scan the room, and there he is—Julian—standing a few feet away, his laughter ringing out like a familiar melody. The sound alone making me weak.

As if he can hear my thoughts through the commotion between us, his eyes lock onto mine, and for a heartbeat, the world around us fades.

Heat creeps up my neck, and I quickly look away. It's been far too long since the last time we spoke, and so much has changed. Like the fact that I've decided to stay in Haven and help Dad with his recovery. I can't help but feel the weight of what that could mean for us. If it's even what he wants.

"Long time no see," Julian says, appearing beside me, his voice low and smooth, cutting through the chatter like a knife.

. . .

"And here I thought you'd forgotten all about me," I blurt out, trying not to sound as desperate as I feel.

He raises an eyebrow, clearly taken aback. "I'm pretty certain forgetting you is impossible, Lina, especially after spending twelve years failing miserably at it."

For a moment, it's just the two of us in a bubble of tension, heat, and unspoken truths. I swallow hard, unsure of how to respond.

"And what if you didn't have to try to forget me?"

He steps closer, the warmth radiating from him sending my heart into a wild spiral. "What do you mean?" he asks.

"I mean... you should ask me out."

"I should?"

"Or not. I'm just saying I'll be around."

"For how long, Lina?" His gaze intensifies, making me so nervous I have to look away.

"I don't know." I stare down at the ground. "This place is growing on me. And you guys do have an Outback now, so..."

He reaches out, grasping my chin and tilting my face up to meet his eyes.

"You're staying?"

"Yes," I admit, my voice barely above a whisper.

He stares back at me, nodding as a slow smile spreads across his lips. I can't help myself; I lean in, my eyes fluttering shut as his lips brush mine, and just when I think he's going to kiss me, he shifts back.

"Hold that thought," he says, suddenly breaking the spell I'd been caught under.

"What?" I ask, confused as he steps back.

"Just something I need to do real quick," he replies, glancing over his shoulder. "Wait right here, okay?"

Before I can respond, he turns away, walking straight to my dad. My stomach squeezes into a tight knot as I watch the determination in Julian's stride. He pulls my dad away from his group of friends. I can't hear their conversation, but it's obvious they're talking about me, especially as they glance in my direction just as Mom pops up with Zorro in her arms.

"I see you're making yourself right at home," she says, a teasing smile on her face.

"No idea what you're talking about," I reply, taking Zorro from her and squeezing him to my chest.

"The guy you were practically falling over. He's cute."

"Shh," I hiss, glancing back at Julian.

"What do you think, Zorro? Do you finally get a daddy?" Mom laughs, rubbing the spot under his chin.

Zorro replies with a loud meow, making me giggle just as Julian starts walking back toward us.

"You can go now, Mom," I say under my breath, bumping her shoulder.

"Oh, I'm most definitely staying," she insists.

. . .

"Mom—"

"Hi, you must be..." She immediately stretched her arm out for Julian to shake, fishing for any bit of information she can get from him.

"Julian," he replies, extending his hand to shake hers.

"I'm Karolina's mother. I've heard nothing about you, so please fill me in since my only daughter won't."

"Unfortunately, not a whole lot to share, but I'm hoping we can change that," he says, smiling as his eyes lock on mine.

Mom smiles, pleased. "I hope so." she says winking at me."

"Can you give us a minute, please, mother,"

"Julian, be good to her,"

"I think this town will be good for you," she whispers in my ear as she kisses my cheek before walking away.

"Who's this?" Julian asks, petting Zorro on the top of his head.

. . .

"Your newest neighbor, Zorro. Now, what were you talking to my dad about?"

"You."

"Obviously," I quip.

"I asked him for permission to date you."

I can't help the laugh that bursts out. "I'm sorry, what?"

"It's important to me that he's cool with this."

"And if he would have said no?"

"No use in wasting time on what-ifs, Lina." He leans down, pressing his forehead to mine. "He said yes, and you said you're staying. That's all that matters to me right now. We'll figure the rest out but for now..." My lips buzz with the anticipation of feeling his lips on mine. "Welcome home, Lina." He leans down, capturing my lips in a kiss that feels just like coming home.

The End

About the Author

K. Rodriguez is a proud Dominican-American writer of sweet and spicy contemporary romance con sazón!

A born-and-raised Jersey girl, she's now soaking up the sun in SW Florida with her high school sweetheart, three kids, and four fur babies. When she's not wrangling children or poodles, you can find her avoiding the laundry, indulging in far too much cafecito, and blasting her old-school playlist like it's still 2003! Besides her love for Aventura, she's an avid romance reader, passionate about real love that navigates the beautiful chaos of life.

instagram.com/k.rodriguezwrites
facebook.com/krodwrites
amazon.com/author/k.rodriguez